About This Book

Waa'aka' is a telling of a creation story from the Tongva, who have lived in Southern California for thousands of years. It takes place on the island of Pimu, just off the Southern California coast. Illustrator Carly Lake was inspired after hearing the narrative, and she created a series of watercolor images that, together with the text, resulted in this book.

This telling includes a couple words in the Tongva language. Those words are *ehee*, which means "yes," and *shaxaat*, which means "willow."

This book is partly inspired by my father. An ocean man and a skin diver, with memories embedded deep in the landscape of our beautiful California, he reminded me to pay attention to the details of nature, and to share them.

Carly and I lovingly dedicate this book to the island of Pimu and the night-night water chick.

—Cindi Alvitre

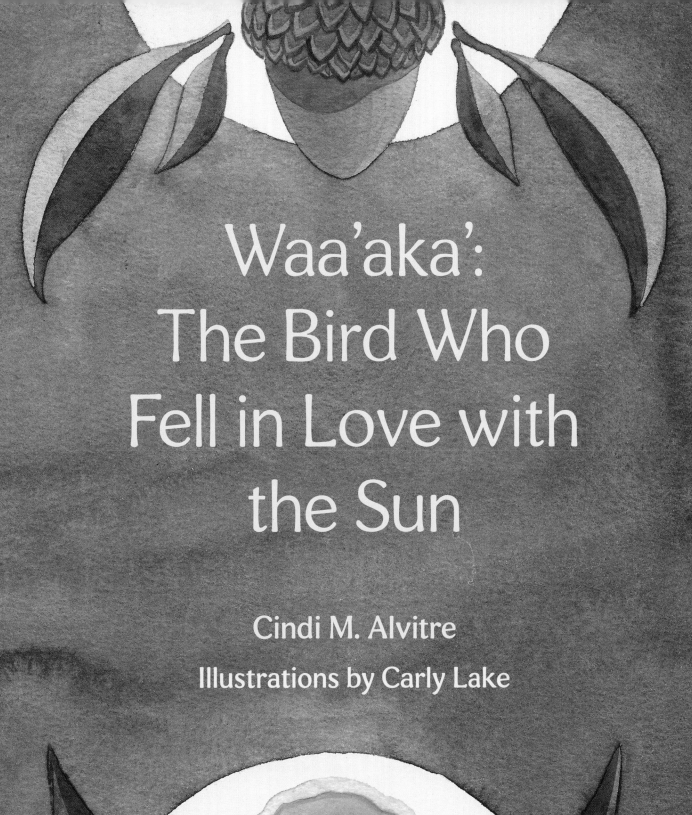

Waa'aka':
The Bird Who
Fell in Love with
the Sun

Cindi M. Alvitre

Illustrations by Carly Lake

Waa'aka' was born when the earth was soft and the waters were new. It was the beginning of time. One day Wiyot, our creator, sat at the edge of the quiet, empty world. He felt very lonely. He thought, "I need to fill this place."

Wiyot had many powers and could do many things.
He took sand in his hand, and he blew it to the four directions.
The grains of sand touched the earth, and they
turned into leaves. Plants began to grow.

The first plant was a giant tree full of acorns. "*Ehee*," said
Wiyot. "Your name will be Oak and your fruit will feed all."

The second was a smaller tree with leaves of gray and
silver. Wiyot named this tree White Sage.

"You will be medicine that all might use for good,"
Wiyot said with respect.

The third tree had branches that kissed the earth when the wind blew.
This one Wiyot named Willow. "*Shaxaat* will shelter all from cold," he said.

The last plant, golden as the sun, brought beauty to the world.
Wiyot named it Island Poppy.

Wiyot watched with joy as his magic came alive.

But Wiyot did more. He dipped his hands into the ocean
and mixed red earth with the water.

Then the winged ones came.

Owl came first, for she saw in the dark when no one else could.

Then came Kingfisher, who promised to be honest and loyal to Wiyot.

Raven came next, dark and noble, and a good listener.

Last was Waa'aka', sleek and beautiful.
Her white feathers glowed like pearls in sand,
and she became Wiyot's favorite.

Yet, even with these creations,
the Earth was still cold and dark.

So Wiyot asked Island Poppy for light.

Island Poppy pulled a petal from her crown,

and a spark of gold flashed in the dark.

Wiyot mixed the petal with a ball of soil.

As he rolled it in his hand, it grew larger

than all the other creations.

Tamet, the sun, was born.

Tamet shone the brightest of them all,
and he was kind and caring to everyone.

He and Waa'aka' became friends.

One day Tamet and Waa'aka' went walking and found a pond.

As they sat at the edge, Tamet gazed at Waa'aka'.

He was falling in love with her.

But she didn't notice him. She was too busy looking at herself

in the water. She thought, "Oh, how beautiful I am;

more beautiful than anyone else!"

Each day Waa'aka' made Tamet come to the water so she could admire her own beauty. Soon she forgot about everyone else.

She even refused to work! "I can't go pick acorns," she'd say. "I might dirty my beautiful white feathers!"

The others saw these changes.
They also saw a change in Tamet.

He was growing larger and rounder and
hotter—so hot that the water dried up,
and so did the leaves on the trees.

Wiyot and Tamet went to their council to talk about this problem, as this was the way it was done back then.

"If we don't do something," the council said to Tamet, "we'll all die from your heat. We have to send you up to the sky. Then you can still be with us, but you will not harm us."

It made Tamet sad to think about leaving, but he also felt for his brothers and sisters. "I must travel to the heavens. But how?"

Owl, full of wisdom, said, "Let's weave a net out of fibers from the plants. Then we can gather around the net and toss Tamet into the heavens!"

They all agreed . . . except for Waa'aka'. She shouted, "How can you take him from me? Without him near, how will I see my beauty? *He is mine*!"

The others cried out, "Waa'aka', what has happened to you? You were once so beautiful, but your vanity has made you ugly!"

And Wiyot said to Waa'aka', "You must help your brothers and sisters, not hurt them! Tamet will go."

But Waa'aka' did not want to give up Tamet.
So she made a secret plan.

The next day, everyone gathered by the water.
They each held part of the net they had woven,
and they placed Tamet in the center.

Waa'aka' pretended to help. But she would not let Tamet go! She would hold on to him as he was tossed into the sky. "Then," she thought, "I will always be with him, and everyone will see me in his great light forever. That will show them!"

They tossed Tamet up, and he flew to one side of the sky and came
back down. They tried again, and this time Tamet flew
to the center of the sky before he fell to Earth.

The third time they put more strength into it, heaving him high. He
floated for a moment, then fell once more. They kept going, lifting
with all their might, tossing Tamet high above them.

As they lifted the net one last time, Waa'aka' held on to Tamet, and they rose together. But as they entered the heavens, Tamet grew much larger than he had been on Earth. It was too hot for Waa'aka'! She fell from the sky, her beautiful white feathers burned black.

The others looked up, amazed. Not only did Tamet stay in the sky, but the net that carried him turned into a million stars that gave even more light and warmth.

They were pleased, but not with Waa'aka'. Wiyot turned to her and said, "Because you were selfish, you will not see the light of Tamet. You will sleep by day, and only by night can you come out, so that Grandmother Moon can watch over you."

To this day, we can see the dark feathers of Waa'aka' as she sits upon the waters at night, waiting for the light of Grandmother Moon so she may gaze at herself.

This is the only light she will ever know.
She is the Black Crowned Night Heron.

About the Author

Cindi Alvitre is a mother and grandmother, and she has been an educator and artist-activist for over three decades. She is a descendant of the original inhabitants of Los Angeles and Orange Counties. In 1985, she and Lorene Sisquoc cofounded Mother Earth Clan, a collective of Indian women who created a model for cultural and environmental education. In the late 1980s she cofounded Ti'at Society, sharing in the renewal of ancient maritime practices of the coastal and island Tongva. She currently teaches American Indian Studies at California State University, Long Beach.

About the Illustrator

Carly Lake is an artist, illustrator, and art educator. Her illustrations have been published in magazines, storyboards, comics, and the chapter book *Candice Can Go*. She lives and makes art near the San Gabriel Mountains in Los Angeles, CA. She invites you to explore more of her work at carlylake.com.